Joey and the
Giant Box

KAR-BEN PUBLISHING
A division of Lerner Publishing Group, Inc.
241 First Avenue North
Minneapolis, MN 55401 USA
1-800-4-KARBEN

Website address: www.karben.com

Main body text set in Chaloops Regular 16/22.
Typeface provided by Chank.

Library of Congress Cataloging-in-Publication Data

Lakritz, Deborah.
      Joey and the giant box / by Deborah Lakritz ; illustrated by Mike Byrne.
          p.   cm.
      Summary: With the help of his friends—and one large discarded box—Joey turns his love of
collecting into a tzedakah, or act of charity, for the local food pantry.
      ISBN 978-1-4677-1953-7 (lib. bdg. : alk. paper)
      [1. Boxes—Fiction. 2. Sharing—Fiction. 3. Charity—Fiction. 4. Collectors and collecting—
Fiction. 5. Jews—United States—Fiction.] I. Byrne, Mike, 1979- illustrator. II. Title.
PZ7.L15934Jo 2015
[E]—dc23   2014003603

Manufactured in the United States of America
1 – DP – 12/31/14

Joey and the Giant Box

Deborah Lakritz

illustrations by
Mike Byrne

KAR-BEN
PUBLISHING

"Mommy, look in our driveway!" said Joey one morning, leaping over his rock collection.

"Don't trip over your marbles. Or your bottle caps. Or your race cars," she warned.

Outside, a long truck vroomed to a stop in front of their garage. Down climbed two men in uniforms.

BW BEST WASHER

"Our new dishwasher is finally here," said Mommy. "Let's show them where it goes."

Joey skipped behind the delivery man as he wheeled an enormous box inside.

"That's the biggest box ever!
Wait 'til I tell my friends at school!"

Once the new dishwasher stood in place,
Mommy turned to Joey.
"Help me carry this box down the driveway.
The recycling truck comes tomorrow."

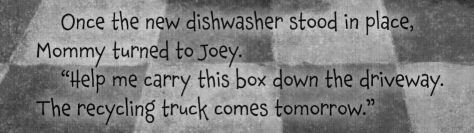

"Give it away?" Joey pleaded. "Can't I **please** keep it?"

"Joey, where will you ever put this gigantic box?" she said, as he started dragging it upstairs to his bedroom.

"Next to my little dinosaurs. And my bouncy balls. And all of my dreidels."

So Joey and Mommy shoved the carton through the door and jammed it into his crowded room.

Joey loved his box!
Some days, he stuffed it full of pillows and—**ta da!**—it became a fort.

Some days, he wore his bicycle helmet and boots, and—poof!—it became a spaceship.

But every day it filled up Joey's entire room.

In the mornings, Joey could barely squeeze out of his room to come downstairs for breakfast.

In the evenings, Mommy and Daddy could barely squeeze in to read him a bedtime story. One night, Joey bumped into the box and sent his marble collection tumbling to the floor.

The next day, Mommy saw the mess and frowned. "I'm sorry, sweetie, but your room is becoming a hazard. When the recycling truck comes tomorrow, the box must go."

Joey's eyes darted around. He tried stuffing the box into his closet.

He tried shoving it under his bed. Mommy was right. The box was just too big for his room.

"Come shopping with me," Mommy said. "Maybe we can find something else for you to collect."

"What's eating you today, Joey-the-Collector?" Ernie asked at the grocery counter.

"My new box," Joey sighed. "Mommy says I have to get rid of it—it's ginormous!"

"As big as **that** one?" Ernie pointed to the wall.

NEIGHBORS HELPING NEIGHBORS

Joey gasped. There stood a cardboard carton just like his. Pictures of peanut butter jars and cans of soup were taped on the front. A banner above it said "NEIGHBORS HELPING NEIGHBORS."

"Wow!" exclaimed Joey. "That box must weigh a ton!" He jumped up and tried to look inside. Then Ernie came over and lifted him up. "Why is there food in there?" he asked.

Ernie explained. "People put food in there for families who don't have enough to eat. When the box is full, a truck will deliver it to a food pantry where hungry people can take what they need."

"There are people who don't have enough to eat?" Joey asked.

His mother nodded, then handed Joey a can of peaches to put inside.

That afternoon, Joey pretended he was at the market, and filled his box with food from their pantry.

Food Bank

"Please don't recycle my box yet," he told his parents at dinner. "I want to collect food for hungry people—just like at the grocery store."

So Mommy called Joey's teacher, Mrs. Winkler, and told her about Joey's big box. She called her friend Mrs. Schutkin at the Star of David Food Pantry. And the next morning Joey and Mommy carried the box into Joey's classroom.

אבגדהוזחטיכדל

"Your box sure is ginormous!" squealed Joey's friends.

"Now it's **our** box," he said, telling everyone about the one at the grocery store and how it helps hungry people.

"And we can bring in stuff like soup and peanut butter to fill it up."

Food Bank

During art, the class cut out pictures of food to glue on the sides of the carton.

Others made posters to hang in the halls, so everyone in the school would know to bring in food. Mrs. Winkler handed the children flyers to take home to their parents.

Every morning, Joey raced
to his classroom and peeked
in to see how the box was
filling up. There were bags
of beans and rice. Jars of
peanut butter and jelly.

Cans of soup and boxes of macaroni. Ernie delivered a trunk full of cereal from the grocery store.

Before long, Joey's collection reached the top of the box. It was time to call the Food Bank.

The next morning during class, a big truck pulled up in front of the school. Two men got out and pushed a dolly toward the entrance.

"They're here for our box!" the children exclaimed.

Star of David Food Bank

After the box had been taken away, Mrs. Winkler called the children together. "I know you will miss your big box," she said, "so here is a much smaller box that can still do a big mitzvah." And she handed each child a colorful box with a Jewish Star printed on the side.

"Drop a coin in here whenever you can," she told the children. "Once it's full you can take the money to Ernie's store and buy swirly noodles and bags of beans and peanut butter and jelly for the Food Pantry."

Joey raised his new little box and smiled. "And this one will even fit in my room!"

About the Author
Deborah Lakritz has a Masters Degree in Social Work from the University of Minnesota. She lives in Milwaukee, Wisconsin, with her husband, five children and pet fish, Sunny. Her previous picture books include *Say Hello, Lily.*

About the Illustrator
Mike Byrne grew up near Liverpool, U.K., and then moved to London to work as an illustrator by day and a crayon wielding crime fighter by night. He now lives with his wife and two cats in the countryside. He spends his days doodling and creating children's books fueled only by tea and cookies.